OUT OF THIS WORLD

Out of This World is published by Stone Arch Books,
A Capstone Imprint
1710 Roe Crest Drive
North Mankato, Minnesota 56003
www.mycapstone.com

Library of Congress Cataloging-in-Publication Data
Names: Bean, Raymond, author.
Title: Journey to the Moon / by Raymond Bean.
Description: North Mankato, Minnesota : Stone Arch Books, an imprint of
Capstone Press, [2016] | Series: Out of this world, out of this world | Summary:
Ten-year-old Starr has decided that living in a space station is cool, but now that it
is time to take a family of space tourists on a trip to the moon she has to cope with
her bossy thirteen-year-old brother, Apollo, who claims it is dangerous for girls--
but when Apollo and the boys he is escorting disappear it is up to Starr to figure
out where they are. Identifiers: LCCN 2016013784| ISBN 9781496536167 (library
binding) | ISBN 9781496536204 (pbk.) | ISBN 9781496536280 (ebook pdf)
Subjects: LCSH: Space stations--Juvenile fiction. | Space tourism--Juvenile fiction.
| Middle-born children--Juvenile fiction. | Brothers and sisters--Juvenile fiction. |
Families--Juvenile fiction. | Outer space--Juvenile fiction. | Moon--Juvenile fiction.
| CYAC: Space stations--Fiction. | Space tourism--Fiction. | Brothers and sisters--
Fiction. | Family life--Fiction. | Outer space--Fiction. | Moon--Fiction.
Classification: LCC PZ7.B3667 Jo 2016 | DDC 813.6 [Fic] --dc23
LC record available at https://lccn.loc.gov/2016013784

Illustrated by: Matthew Vimislik
Designer: Veronica Scott

Printed and bound in Canada
PO009640FRF16

OUT OF THIS
WORLD

JOURNEY
TO THE
MOON

by Raymond Bean

STONE ARCH BOOKS
a capstone imprint

TABLE OF CONTENTS

INTRODUCTION

My name is Starr. I'm just like every other ten-year-old girl I know, with one major difference: I live in space.

You see, my mom is a world-class astronaut, scientist, and all-around super-genius. She was chosen to be the first person to move her entire family to space. Now she's not just my mom, she's also in charge of the world's most advanced space station.

Dad is a documentary filmmaker. He's making a movie about our family being the first family to ever live in space. It's not like we're actors or anything. He just films us doing our everyday stuff like eating, playing, and brushing our teeth.

I have a thirteen-year-old brother named Apollo. He thinks he's cooler than winter.

Cosmo is my super-cute, five-year-old brother.

If you ask me, he *is* cooler than winter. We call him "Cozzie" for short.

We're helping lead the new world of space tourism so that people can take vacations to space. I like to call them space-cations.

The head of the entire space program is Mrs. Sosa. She's my mom's boss. Her granddaughter, Tia, and I work together. Tia trains kids on Earth to get them ready for space. I help them with life in space once they're on the station.

My best friend, Allison, thinks I'll forget all about her now that I live in space, but just because I live in space doesn't mean I don't need my best friend.

I may be a regular girl, but my life is completely out of this world!

Chapter 1

TOO DANGEROUS FOR GIRLS

Waking up in space is really strange. Your body just floats like you're on pause. I always find myself in the strangest positions. I've awoken upside down, sideways, and spread out like a starfish. This time my arms were floating out in front of me like I was a space zombie.

Through the window of my sleep nook, I could make out the lights glimmering down on Earth. I figured we were orbiting somewhere over Asia.

My phone buzzed. It was my best friend, Allison.

I answered and said, "Hey, Allison."

Her face appeared on the screen.

"Good morning, Starr. Or is it night up there? I never know."

"We're passing over Asia. It's night here, but I'm just waking up."

"Why are you waking up if it's night?" she asked.

"We still follow the time in Colorado."

"So you're over Asia and it's nighttime there, but you're just waking up because it's morning in Colorado?" she asked.

"Yes, I know. It's confusing. You look really pretty, by the way," I said.

"Thanks! It's picture day at school."

"That's exciting!" I said.

"Not as exciting as whatever you have planned, I'm sure," she replied.

"Starr," I heard my little brother, Cozzie, say from somewhere in my room.

"Yes?" I answered.

"Are you awake?" he asked.

I opened the hatch suddenly and smiled at him. "Of course I'm awake, silly."

He smiled back and laughed a little. "Mom said it's time to get up. The meeting starts in ten minutes."

"Allison, I have to go," I said, turning back to my phone. "Have a great time at picture day."

"I will. What are you guys doing today?"

"We're going to the Moon!" Cozzie shouted.

"That's amazing!" Allison replied. "I can't wait to hear all about it. Talk to you guys soon!"

"Bye!" I said, as I waved and hung up.

I changed quickly and floated through the nook's hatch and out into my main pod. "Thanks for waking me up," I said. "Let's go."

Cozzie turned on his cruiser and took off. I clicked mine on and followed. Getting around in space can be really slow. The cruisers help move us through the station quicker. Also, they're super-fun! We zipped out of my pod

and whizzed through a long tube that led to the meeting pod.

The entire crew attends morning meetings to go over the events planned for the day. It looked as if everyone was already there. Mom and Dad were talking with Mrs. Sosa on a big video monitor when we arrived. "Good morning, Starr and Cozzie," she said.

Cozzie waved.

"Good morning, Mrs. Sosa," I said. "How are things on Earth?"

Tia's face appeared next to Mrs. Sosa's. "Not as good as they are in space, I bet," she said. I tried not to roll my eyes, but the way Mom looked at me made me think I might have.

Tia and Mrs. Sosa live in a desert at the space-training center. They've been to the space station before, but Tia wishes they could live here full time, as my family does.

"Good morning, Starr," Mom said. "We were just about to get started."

"Hey, the gang's all here," Dad said, as my older brother, Apollo, zoomed in on his cruiser. Dad clicked a fresh battery into his video recorder. He lifted his camera and said, "Okay, everyone, recording in three, two, one, action!"

"Good news, we're on schedule for the first group of space tourists to arrive in a few days," Mrs. Sosa said. "Tia has been working really hard to prepare the group's children. They're all very excited to make the trip to space."

"We're ready for their arrival and looking forward to it," Mom said. "Also, as you know, today is our first Moon landing! The station is currently orbiting the Moon, and we're close enough to get there in a short amount of time. We'll explore the surface, check to make sure the equipment is in working order, and prepare for the big Moon walk with the guests next week."

"Sounds like a plan," Mrs. Sosa said. Mrs. Sosa and Mom continued talking about the details, but I couldn't focus. I was too excited. I felt like I might burst. We'd been planning our first trip to the Moon for weeks. I couldn't wait to finally get down there and check it out.

"The Moon is going to be so amazing!" I whispered to Apollo.

"You're not really going down with us, are you? You're too young," he whispered back. "And you're a girl. It's not safe for girls."

I couldn't believe my ears. *What makes him think it's safe for boys, but not girls?* I wondered. "Mom is a girl," I reminded him.

"Mom's a *woman*, and she's a scientist. You'd never make it on the Moon. Do you know that only twelve people have ever walked on the Moon? They were all men."

"Guys, we're in the middle of a meeting, and I'm recording here," Dad whispered.

"Am I going to the Moon today too?" I asked.

"Of course you are," Dad said.

I glanced at Apollo. "Apollo said I'm too young, and it's

too dangerous for girls," I said, speaking loudly enough for everyone to hear.

"Apollo! That's ridiculous. Apologize to your sister," Mom said.

He looked at me reluctantly. "I'm sorry."

"Thank you," Mom said. She turned back to her conversation with Mrs. Sosa.

When Mom wasn't looking, Apollo whispered, "I'm sorry that the Moon's too dangerous for girls."

Chapter 2

HOLDING HANDS
ON THE MOON

Later that day, we were finally orbiting the Moon. I was looking out of the window and talking to Tia at the same time.

"Apollo thinks the Moon is too dangerous for girls," I said. "Can you believe that?"

"Did he forget that this girl trained him to live in space?" Tia asked.

"I know!" I said. We both shook our heads in disbelief.

"You're so lucky!" she whined suddenly. "I can't believe you're about to be the first girl ever to land on the Moon. You have to remember every single detail. I need to know everything."

"Dad already mounted video cameras on our helmets. They'll record everything we see and stream the video back to Earth," I said.

"I know. My grandmother said we'd be able to see the video down here, but it's not the same. I want to go too!"

"Aren't you coming back up when we take the guests on the Moon walk next week?" I asked.

"Yes, but I want to be up there today," she pouted.

I wished Tia wasn't so jealous of me for living in space.

My phone buzzed. It was a text from Mom.

It read: *We're about to leave. Where are you?*

"I have to go! I'll talk with you later."

"Have fun," she said unconvincingly.

After hanging up, I quickly put on my space suit and raced toward the garage to meet the family.

Mom, Dad, Apollo, and Cozzie were already in the spaceship when I arrived. I floated in through the hatch in the roof and buckled in next to Cozzie in the backseat.

"We were starting to wonder where you were," Dad said.

"I was talking with Tia."

"Were you having second thoughts?" Apollo asked. "It's not too late to change your mind if you're afraid."

"Sounds like you're the one who's afraid," I replied.

"Why would either of you be afraid?" Mom asked. "We're going to be perfectly safe on the Moon. Apollo — leave your sister alone."

"I'm just saying that if she's afraid, she doesn't have to go on the Moon walk," Apollo sulked.

"We're going to be the first family to land on the Moon. Why would she want to miss that?" Dad asked.

Apollo just shrugged. "No reason."

"Why are there cameras on our helmets?" Cozzie asked suddenly, pointing to the one on my helmet.

Dad said, "Going to the Moon is a really big deal. People haven't set foot on it since 1972. It's important that we stream video of our Moon walk back to Earth for everyone to see."

"Is it going to be on TV?" Cozzie asked.

"Probably," Dad said. "I'm sure the story will be in the papers and the video will be all over the Internet too."

The large exit hatch opened on the side of the station, and our ship blasted out.

The Moon looked as if it was glowing against the black of space.

"I heard only twelve people have ever been to the Moon," I said.

Dad took out his video camera and clicked it on. "Can you repeat that, Starr? I'd love to get it in my film."

I repeated what I'd said. Dad gave me a thumbs-up and kept recording.

"Dad's right," Mom said to me. "It's a big deal. I will be the first woman to ever set foot on the Moon."

". . . and me, Starr, and Apollo will be the first kids to ever go to the Moon?" Cozzie asked.

"That's right!" replied Dad.

"Awesome!" Cozzie exclaimed.

I had seen pictures of the Moon before, but seeing it in real life, as we got closer and closer, was out of this world! I took a picture and texted it to Allison. Thankfully the technology on the station made it easy to text and call Earth.

We were flying pretty high above the surface, but I could easily make out mountains and craters below. Some of the mountains were way higher than I would have ever imagined. Everything was mainly grays, blacks, and whites. I glanced back over my shoulder to see Earth. I thought about all the water, trees, and life on my home planet. The Moon was completely the opposite. It looked like a gigantic gray desert.

"It's covered with circles," Cozzie announced.

"Those are spots where asteroids and comets and things smashed into the Moon a long time ago. They're called craters," Apollo said.

"Is anything going to smash into it while we're there?" Cozzie asked.

"No," I answered. "Most of what you see happened a long time ago. If anything dangerous were coming toward us, the crew on the station would see it coming on satellites and warn us before it could hurt us."

"Actually, small space debris is hard to see using satellites and can strike at any time," added Apollo. "We should be fine, but you never know."

"We're perfectly safe," Mom reassured Cozzie. "It's very unlikely that anything would strike the Moon." She glared at Apollo.

My body was shaking a little because I was so excited. I could feel my teeth chattering as if I was really cold.

We cruised past endless craters, mountains, and

flat areas covered in more gray dust. Even though it all looked pretty much the same, it was fascinating.

Mom landed the ship, hovering carefully above the surface as if it were a helicopter. We touched down slowly and softly on the surface. She turned off the engine, and we were all perfectly silent. I don't think I've ever experienced such stillness. Nothing moved outside the windows. There was no life, no wind, no rain, nothing but the Moon as far as I could see in every direction.

"Okay, my little Moontonians," Mom said unbuckling. "Let's go play. You've been living in Zero-G and are used to weightlessness. Remember, now that we're on the surface of the Moon, it'll be more similar to Earth. However, don't forget that gravity is about six times weaker here than on Earth. Everything will feel lighter. You'll be able to move around easier, and it will take a little getting used to. Take it slow at first and get used to the feeling."

"Can I go out first?" Apollo asked.

"I hadn't really thought about it," Mom admitted.

"You should go first," Dad said to Mom, squeezing her hand. "This is your mission."

"This is our mission," she said, turning to all of us.

"Why don't we all hold hands and jump out together, like we're jumping into a pool?" Cozzie asked.

"I love that idea," I said.

"Me too!" Mom and Dad exclaimed together.

"But why can't I go first?" Apollo asked again. "The last missions to the Moon were called the Apollo missions after all."

"Yes, but this Moon landing is a family mission," Mom said.

"Let's all be on our best behavior," Dad said, looking at Apollo and clicking off his video camera. "I'm turning on the helmet cameras now. We're live from the Moon in three, two, one, ACTION!"

Chapter 3

NO DRIVER'S LICENSE NEEDED

Before we went out, Mom and Dad checked our helmets to make sure they were on correctly. Then Mom pressed a button that opened a large air lock on the side of the ship. We all unbuckled from our seats and stood on the edge of the ship, looking out on the Moon.

"WOW!" I exclaimed.

"Cozzie, would you like to count down from five?" Mom asked.

He nodded and counted, "Five, four, three, two, one . . ."

"Jump!" Mom shouted.

We all jumped from the edge and sailed out of the ship. On Earth we would have had a hard time jumping more than six inches in our space suits, but on the Moon we floated up about three feet. I moved my feet as if I were a cartoon character trying to run in midair. The rest of the family did it too.

From the ship to the ground, it was a pretty soft landing. If we had landed from that height on Earth, it would have really hurt.

Soft, powder-like dust covered the surface. Every step made a footprint. "There isn't any wind or rain on the Moon, so your footsteps will be here for years and years to come," Mom said.

Dad bounced past me. He looked a lot like a kangaroo hopping along. I couldn't believe how far he was able to travel in one hop. Mom was right. It looked about six times as far as he could do it on Earth. "Wait for me!" I shouted, bending my knees and taking a giant leap forward. I launched myself off the ground and landed way farther than where I thought I would. I hopped again and traveled even farther.

By the time we finally stopped, we had moved pretty far from the ship. "We should probably head back," Dad said. "We don't want to get lost."

We turned around and I started skipping instead of kangaroo hopping. It worked even better, and I pulled ahead of Dad. Since it worked so well, he started skipping too. He looked pretty funny doing it. He caught up to me, and I grabbed hold of his hand. We skipped together all the way back to the ship.

Cozzie, Apollo, and Mom watched. They were all laughing pretty hard.

"This is the coolest thing ever!" Apollo said.

"Hold that thought," Mom said. "I'll be right back." She bounced over to the ship and disappeared inside.

"What's she doing?" Cozzie asked.

"I don't know," I said.

I heard a humming sound and noticed a ramp slowly lowering from the far back of the ship. Once it was all the way to the ground, a four-wheeled cart rolled down the ramp with Mom behind the wheel. She drove over to us and stopped.

"Who wants to go for a ride?" she asked. It had four seats and, before I could even answer, Apollo was in the front seat. Dad and I hopped in the back, and Cozzie sat on Dad's lap.

"This Moon rover is going to help us travel across the Moon's surface with ease," Mom said. "We'll be able to explore places people have never been and give our guests the adventure of a lifetime." Mom pressed on the gas. We bounced along laughing, and I realized that I couldn't stop smiling. It seemed as if every time I did something absolutely amazing, there was something even more amazing about to happen.

Mom drove us to the top of a hill and stopped. "Apollo, do you want to drive?" she asked.

"Really?" he asked

"Why not, there's not a driving age on the Moon, and there's very little traffic," Mom said, giving us a wink. "Starr, would you like to drive after him?"

"You bet!" I said.

Suddenly I heard a ringing. A small image of Tia appeared in the lower corner of my helmet.

"I think I'm getting a call from Tia," I announced.

"Go ahead," Mom instructed. "Just say 'answer' and you'll be able to see her and talk to her."

"Answer," I said, and the image of Tia turned to a live video. "Starr? Can you see me?" she asked.

"Yeah, in the corner of the glass inside my helmet. Can you see me?"

"I can see you fine. I wanted to check the video-calling to make sure it worked on the Moon. How's it going up there?"

"It's totally amazing. I can't wait for you to try it."

"The video from your helmets is incredible!" said Tia.

"You are so LUCKY! I wish I were up there now!"

"Sorry," I said, but I wasn't sure what I was apologizing for. It wasn't my fault that my mom was selected by Mrs. Sosa to go to space.

"Grandma also wanted me to check in with you and make sure all your equipment is working well," Tia added.

"Yeah, everything is great."

"Starr, it's your turn to drive," Mom said.

"I've got to go," I said to Tia.

"OMG! You're going to drive the Moon rover! That's my ultimate dream! You are so lucky!!"

I tried not to roll my eyes, but I think I did. Mom says it's a bad habit of mine. I couldn't help it. "We can ride in it together when you come up."

"It won't be the same," she said.

"Do you want to stay on the video chat while I drive?" I asked.

"No, I should go. I can hardly take it," she said, looking

disappointed. "You have fun." She clicked off the video call without even saying goodbye. I thought it was kind of rude of her to just hang up like that, but that was Tia.

"Everything okay?" Mom asked.

I wanted to tell Mom how I really felt, but then I remembered that the video was streaming on our helmets and Tia was watching. I just nodded.

I felt that Tia had called just to make me feel guilty about being on the Moon. It was pretty unfair of her.

I got over it pretty quickly, though, because Apollo was right: driving the rover was the coolest thing ever!

Chapter 4

SPACE-CATION

A few days later, I was playing in my room with Cozzie when I looked out my window and saw a huge ship coming toward us.

"The guests are here!" Cozzie shouted.

We grabbed our cruisers and zoomed out of my room, down the tube, and into the kitchen. Mom, Dad, and the rest of the crew waited there, looking just as excited as we were.

Professor Will piloted the guests up from Earth, and he was the first one to enter the station. Behind him, a floating parade of people followed — the kids first, and then the adults. I counted two boys and two girls. They looked a little frightened as they pulled themselves toward us, along the stabilizer bars.

When they were all inside, Professor Will floated to the center and spoke to the crowd. "Ladies and gentlemen, on behalf of all of us at the station, I'd like to welcome you to our space home and wish you a safe stay." Everyone applauded. Some people twisted to one side or another, trying to keep in control. A few even lost control of their body, ending up upside down and sideways. Everyone smiled as they struggled with how to stay in control. "Now, I'd like to introduce you to the head of the station."

Mom floated forward. "Congratulations on becoming the world's very first space tourists!" she said. Everyone clapped again. "My family and crew are thrilled about your visit and can't wait to show you an out-of-this-world experience. You've all been assigned a team leader who will be your contact person while you're on the ship.

Please take the rest of today to get settled in. We hope you're as excited as we are to take you on the first-ever space-cation to the Moon."

The grown-ups applauded again, then erupted into conversation. It was like a floating party. Having all the other people on the ship was kind of weird.

Mom floated over with a little girl and her mother. The girl had pin-straight hair like mine, only hers was deep-space black. She looked about my age. "Starr, this is Valiente. She's been training with Tia and will be on your team during her stay."

"Hi, I'm Starr," I said. "You have a beautiful name."

"'Valiente' means 'courageous' in Spanish," her mom said proudly.

"My friends call me Val for short," she said. "I'm not feeling very courageous right now, though. If I'm honest, I'm kind of terrified."

"Don't be," I said. "It's completely safe up here. You'll get used to it in no time."

"I don't know," she said, widening her eyes and pointing out toward Earth in the distance. "We're pretty high up, and so far from home."

"Once you get used to it, it feels perfectly normal." I smiled at her. "You'll see." Mom had said I'd be like a teacher when the guests arrived, and now I knew why. Valiente was scared, and part of my job was to make her feel safe.

"Why don't you show Val around the station?" Mom suggested, squeezing my hand. "I'll go get the other member of your team," she said, floating off.

"That's a good idea," Val's mother said. "Why don't you take the tour and get to know the girls? I'll meet you back here in a little while."

"We can take my cruiser," I said. "It's the best way to get around the station." I pulled it from my back and turned it on. "We can stop by the tech pod and get one for you too."

Mom returned with another girl and her parents. A

girl with long, dark hair that spiraled up in tight curls said, "I'm Monique."

"I'm Starr," I said.

"I know. Tia told me all about you," she said.

"Can I take a picture of you guys?" Monique's mom asked.

"Sure," I said.

We all huddled together, our hair lifting up wildly, and smiled. All the moms took pictures on their phones. Monique's mom showed us the picture and we laughed. It felt really good to have other kids on the station.

"Why don't you show the girls around? I'll get their parents settled in," Mom said.

"If it's not too much trouble," Monique said to both Mom and me.

"Yeah, if you don't mind," Val added, smiling.

"I'm here to make sure you guys have a good trip." I smiled at them. "Hold on to my shoulders," I instructed. "You're in for a treat!"

Chapter 5

A FUNNY FEELING

Val held on to me and Monique held on to Val, creating a long chain, and we took off. I didn't go as fast as I'm used to going, but I could tell they were having fun by the way they were giggling.

We cruised out of the pod and through a tube that led back to my room. At an intersection, we almost crashed into Apollo and the boys I'd seen earlier. They were all hanging on to him in the same way the girls were holding on to me. I had to swerve wildly to avoid a crash.

We floated in the intersection where the tubes meet.

"Watch where you're going," Apollo warned. I could tell he was trying to seem cool in front of the new boys.

"Apollo, this is Val and Monique," I said, trying to be polite.

"Hey," he said, in his coolest voice. "Welcome to space."

"Thanks," they said.

I waited for him to introduce the boys, but he didn't. So I said, "Hi, I'm Starr. Welcome to the station."

"Hi, I'm Clark," said a tall boy, who looked as if he was around Apollo's age.

"I'm Myles," said a younger-looking boy with freckles and dark glasses.

"We're happy to have you guys on board," I replied. I suddenly felt like an airline stewardess. Mom would have been proud of how welcoming I was being. I couldn't say the same for Apollo. "I'm taking the girls to the tech pod to get cruisers."

"I was going to do the same thing for these guys," Apollo replied. "Let's race!"

"There are more people on board now. Someone could get hurt."

"No one is going to get hurt. If you're afraid to race the guys' team, just say so." He said it as if it were a challenge, which I didn't appreciate.

"I'm not afraid. I just don't think it's safe."

"Whatever," he said and took off. The other boys held on and trailed behind.

"Sorry about my brother. He's really competitive."

"Clark is my brother," Val said. "He's really competitive too. They're going to get along great or get each other in a lot of trouble."

We cruised into the tech pod. The new boys already had their cruisers and were coming out. They almost crashed into us again!

"Careful!" Professor Will called out from the tech pod.

"All of a sudden, Apollo's acting like the cool kid," I said to him.

"Well, it won't be cool when he crashes into something

and gets hurt," Professor Will replied. "Anyway, I have your cruisers all ready for you. Help yourselves."

The girls grabbed a cruiser each.

We cruised slowly through the station to my pod. It was a clear night and the lights of South America were on display below.

"This is your room?" Val asked, as we floated in.

"It's the coolest room in the entire solar system," Monique said, taking it all in.

"We call rooms pods. Mine is pretty fantastic," I admitted, "but I hardly ever get a chance to share it with anyone." I hadn't realized it until that moment, but I had been feeling kind of lonely. "I'm glad you're all here," I said.

"I'm glad we're here too," Val said, smiling.

"We were afraid you wouldn't like us," Monique added.

"Why wouldn't I like you?" I asked.

The girls glanced at each other as if they had said something they shouldn't have said. "No reason," Val said.

I didn't ask again, but I was confused. I wondered

why they would think I wouldn't like them. I couldn't help think Tia might have something to do with it.

"Watch the Earth," I said, changing the subject. "The line where night meets the daylight is about to appear." We all watched through the clear walls of my pod. Within a few minutes, the line appeared below.

"That's remarkable," Monique said.

"It will be completely light in a little while," I said. "We're moving so fast that we circle Earth about once every ninety minutes. We see a sunrise and a sunset about sixteen times a day."

"How do you know when to go to sleep?" Val asked.

"We still keep track of time using clocks, but it gets confusing without 24-hour days like we're used to on Earth. When it's time to sleep, we close the shades in our sleep hatches so the sunrises don't wake us up. Do you want to see more of the station?" I asked.

They nodded enthusiastically. We zoomed out of my room and into the tube that leads to the aquaponics pod.

Kathy is in charge of all the plants on the station. She was picking some tomatoes when we floated in. I introduced the new girls.

"Hi, everyone," Kathy said. "Welcome! We're very excited to have you aboard." She smiled. "I have lots of work to do, but I'm sure Starr will give you a tour of this amazing pod."

I smiled too. I knew I could do a good job, no matter what Apollo or Tia said.

"In this pod we raise fish and grow all kinds of plants so we can have fresh fruits and vegetables. The fish and the plants rely on each other," I said. "It's called aquaponics."

"Why are the plants growing on top of the fish tanks?" Monique asked.

"The plant roots get moisture from the fish tanks," I said. "The fish waste is also used to give the plants nutrients."

"But why doesn't the water float away?" Monique asked.

"The tanks are completely sealed to keep the water in. Oxygen is pumped into the tanks for the fish," I replied.

"It's pretty amazing," she added.

"We grow tomatoes, lettuce, oranges, and all kinds of other food in here," I said. "We're learning how to make the station completely self-sufficient, so that we don't need any food from Earth."

"Wow! You really know a lot about this stuff!" Val said.

Yeah, I guess I do, I thought. I imagined that Apollo probably hadn't taught the boys anything about the aquaponics lab yet. "Thanks," I said.

I showed them the rest of the plants and even let them feed the fish.

After they each had a turn, we zoomed out of the pod.

We circled back to the kitchen and found some of the moms. When they saw us, they all gathered around.

"This is the most amazing place!" Val exclaimed. "Starr's pod is so unbelievable. There's also a pod full of all kinds of plants and fish. I even got to feed the fish! And Starr . . ."

"Slow down," her mother said, smiling. "It sounds like you two are really hitting it off." She turned to Val and whispered something. I think it was, "I told you that you didn't have anything to worry about."

I wondered what she meant.

Just then Dad appeared on his cruiser. "I'm sorry to break up the party, but I'm going to show everyone to their pods so they can rest. They've had a long day."

"I'll see you tomorrow," I said. "If you need anything, call or message me."

They all thanked me and zoomed off with their families after Dad.

I texted Allison: *Just gave the girls a tour of the station. They're really nice, but I feel like something strange is going on.*

Like what? she asked.

I don't know. I just get a funny feeling, I replied.

Chapter 6

SPACE SHAMPOO

The next morning after breakfast, Cozzie and I picked up the girls from their pods. "I have a lot of activities planned for us today. Are you ready to learn a little more about how we live in space?" I asked.

They nodded.

Part of my job was to show them how we live on the station. Mom said it was important to get as many people to space as possible, especially kids. It was the best way to inspire them to want to explore space. I had so much to show them. I had the whole day planned out.

The girls followed me on their cruisers to the bathroom. "The first thing I want to show you is how we wash our hair in space."

"It's so weird," Cozzie said.

"On Earth, you turn on the water, it flows out of the showerhead, and gravity moves the water down the drain. In space, it's not that simple. Since we're in microgravity, the water doesn't go down. If we were to turn on a shower in space, the water would float."

"What would happen if you tried to take a bath?" Cozzie asked.

The girls and I giggled. "It would be a real mess," I said. "The water would go everywhere."

"To wash your hair, you'll need a pouch of water, a small towel, some shampoo, and a brush." I pointed to all of the items already attached with Velcro to the wall next to me. "First, I squeeze a little water out," I said, showing them how it worked.

The looks on the girls' faces were priceless.

"It's like water balls!" Monique exclaimed. "We saw this a little during training with Tia. I love it!"

I cupped the water balls in my hand and rubbed them into my hair. Two really big ones floated away and I reached out and pulled them back. "Then I take the shampoo and squeeze out a little onto my hair, rubbing it in like this," I said, rubbing the shampoo into my hair. "Then I take my brush and brush it all the way through."

"That's wild!" Val said.

"I can't believe how crazy your hair looks standing up like that when it's wet!" said Monique.

"I use a small amount of water to get the shampoo out of my hair, and then I dry as much of it as I can with a dry cloth. So, let's all give it a try." I opened a bag attached to the wall that had brushes and cloths inside. I gave one to each girl.

The girls washed their hair the best they could. It was a lot of fun watching them get used to handling water in space. By the time we were finished, water balls seemed to be everywhere.

"Can we show them how we brush our teeth?" Cozzie asked, doing a somersault.

"That was my next activity," I said.

I took out my toothbrush and a tube of toothpaste from a ziplock bag attached by Velcro to the wall. They floated in front of me, turning and twisting as if they were floating in water. I wriggled my hands as if I were doing a magic trick. The girls and Cozzie giggled. "The first thing I need to do is squeeze a little toothpaste on the brush just like I would on Earth. Then squeeze a small ball of water out." A few tiny water balls floated in front of me.

I let the water absorb into the brush and then began to brush the same way I would on Earth.

"Now," I said, talking as clearly as possible with a mouth full of toothpaste, "I can't spit out the toothpaste like I would on Earth."

"You swallow it!" Cozzie said gleefully.

"Eww!" the girls said at the same time.

"It's special toothpaste," I said. "You wouldn't want to do that on Earth, but here on the station it's the way we have to do it."

The girls each took a turn brushing their teeth, and then we headed to the kitchen to meet Dad.

"This isn't like my kitchen on Earth," Val said.

"You're right," Dad said. "But we do have some of the things that you have on Earth, such as a microwave. Most of the foods we have are prepackaged for us and we can heat them up."

"Eating in space can be really challenging," I said. "Foods float away all the time and can become really messy. One time I was eating chicken and I got distracted. I found it a few days later floating in one of the tubes."

Dad said, "Every time Cozzie eats, something seems to float away."

"Watch this," I said, taking out a bowl and letting it

float in front of me. Then I opened a container of cereal and attempted to pour the cereal into the bowl. It floated away from the bowl.

"That's so weird!" Monique exclaimed.

"What should we do?" Val asked.

"Eat the cereal!" Cozzie shouted. He floated forward and gobbled up as many pieces of cereal as he could.

The girls and I joined in. I realized it was the first time in a while that I'd played with kids other than my brothers. I felt really thankful to have the girls on board. Also, Val was really good at catching flying cereal!

Chapter 7

FLIPPING OUT

Later, the girls and I were playing in my room. "I can still do lots of the activities that I did on Earth, they're just different." I said. "I think gymnastics is even more fun in space."

"How do you do gymnastics in space?" Val asked.

"I've made up my own version. Let's try it!" I said excitedly. "We can go one at a time. One person makes up a move, and then the others repeat it. Like this." I pushed off the wall and twisted slowly to my left. My body rotated all the way around and I turned into a flip.

"That was unbelievable!" exclaimed Monique.

"It's easy. Now one of you goes," I said.

Monique volunteered first. She pushed off the wall, like I did, and twisted to her left. As she rose up, she slowly flipped and finished on the other side of the pod.

"Wow!" Val said. "Amazing! I don't know if I can do it."

"Just do your best," I said. "It's not about doing it perfectly, it's about having fun."

Val pushed off the wall and shot up like a rocket twisting to her left. She ended up doing three flips before making it to the top. We clapped. She lifted her hands in the air to take a floating bow.

After we all tried our moves at space gymnastics, we moved to my dance studio. "The cool thing about this dance room is that you can dance on the ceiling," I said.

"I can't believe my eyes," Monique said. "It's too crazy!"

"Can we try?" Val asked.

"Of course," I said. It was so much fun to share my room with the girls.

We danced for what seemed like hours.

That night, the girls slept over in my room. We attached sleeping bags to the side of my nook, and they hung in space like flags blowing in the wind.

"What was it like on the Moon?" Monique asked.

"Tell us everything," Val added, pulling herself in closer to me.

"It was amazing. You guys are going to love it," I said. "It reminded me a lot of the desert, but even more empty. There aren't any plants or animals. There aren't any birds, wind, clouds, or rain. There's just space and Moon."

"Were you scared?" Monique asked.

"I was a little scared before we left," I said. "But once we were there, it was so much fun that I forgot all about being scared."

I looked at them. "Are you excited for your Moon walk?" I asked.

The girls looked at each other and went quiet.

"If I'm honest, I don't think I want to go," Val said.

"Me neither," Monique added.

"Why?" I asked. "It's the chance of a lifetime."

"What if something goes wrong down there?" Monique asked.

"We've already done a safety check on all the equipment. You will be perfectly safe," I assured them.

"That's not what we heard," Val admitted.

"Where'd you hear that?" I asked.

They glanced at each other. "I don't get it," I said.

"It was Tia," Monique said, after a long pause.

"She said the Moon walk isn't safe," Val added.

"She said we could float away and drift off into space forever," Monique said. "She really freaked me out."

It explained why the girls had been acting so weird. I wondered why Tia would lie to them about the Moon.

"Why don't we just enjoy our sleepover tonight and we can figure it out in the morning?" I suggested.

"That's a good idea," Val said, "but I'm not going."

"Me neither," Monique said.

Chapter 8

TELL MOM?

In the morning, the girls went back to their pods to get ready for the day. I wasn't sure how to tell Mrs. Sosa about what Tia had said. Mrs. Sosa is in charge of the entire space station. If she got mad at me, it might affect Mom.

I called Allison. She appeared on my phone and said, "Hey, Starr. How's it going with your new visitors?"

I told her about what happened with Tia. "I'm not sure what to do," I said. "If I say something to Mrs. Sosa, she's going to be really upset with Tia. If I don't say anything, it looks like I'm not doing a good job helping the visitors. I'm supposed to be their team leader on the station."

"But it definitely won't look good if the first group of tourists you have on the station chickens out," Allison said.

I hadn't thought of it that way. If the girls didn't want to go on the Moon walk, it might make other people afraid to come to space too.

Apollo cruised in.

"I'll call you later," I said.

"Good luck," Allison said before ending the call.

"We had the best sleepover last night! We were up so late playing dodgeball," Apollo said, placing his cruiser on his back.

"That sounds fun," I said.

"Clark and Myles are really cool. They're pretty lucky to have a team leader like me."

My sleepover didn't go so well, I thought. *Thanks for asking.*

"Apollo, can I trust you with something?"

"Sure," he said. "What is it?" I wasn't sure if I could trust him to take it seriously, but I didn't have anyone else to tell.

"I don't want to worry Mom, and I can't really tell Mrs. Sosa."

"What is it?" he asked, seeming genuinely concerned.

"The girls don't want to go on the Moon walk," I said. "I told them it's completely safe, but they think something bad is going to happen. I'm afraid that if this mission is ruined because the kids won't do this, Mom might get in trouble with Mrs. Sosa."

"Mrs. Sosa and Tia are coming up to the station today," Apollo replied. "You should probably tell Mom that the girls are too afraid to go. Can't say I'm surprised," he smirked.

I wanted to say something about his comment, but I had enough to worry about without getting in an argument with him.

I took a deep breath to calm myself and cruised out of my room. Before I went to Mom, I called Tia.

She answered right away. "Hi, Starr!"

"Hi, Tia. Are you excited to come up today?"

"I can't wait! I've been looking forward to it forever."

"Tia, I have a problem. I'm trying to get the girls ready for the Moon mission, but they're kind of afraid."

"That's weird," she said, avoiding eye contact with me.

"Did they seem afraid before they came up?" I asked.

"No," Tia replied slowly. "They were all ready to go. They couldn't wait. I wonder if something happened up there with you that frightened them."

Was she trying to make it my fault? I wondered. "What time are you getting here?" I asked, changing the subject before I got angry.

"We're taking off in about an hour. We should be there by the end of the day. Do you want me to talk with the girls before I come up?" she asked.

"No!" I insisted. "I'll figure it out." I wished her a

good trip and hung up. Tia was going to ruin the Moon landing if I didn't figure something out quick.

I cruised through the station, following the GPS to where Mom worked. She was fixing the wires on a computer when I arrived.

"Hi, honey," she said. "How's it going with the girls? Is everyone excited for the Moon landing?"

I forced a smile. "They're excited about it," I said, leaving out that they were actually terrified. "We had a good time yesterday and last night. They're really nice."

"That's wonderful! You're doing a great job getting them used to space. Their parents were telling me last night what a fantastic experience the girls are having."

"Thanks," I said.

"The Moon walk is going to be a life-changing experience for all of us. I can't wait."

She was so excited I couldn't bring myself to say anything.

"Did you need something?" she asked.

"No, I just wanted to say good morning. I'll let you get back to work."

I zoomed off. I had to figure something out fast.

Chapter 9

IF YOU INSIST

Tia and Mrs. Sosa arrived later that night. When it was time to greet their ship, I told Mom I was too busy with last-minute preparations.

"I thought you'd be excited to see Tia," she said.

"I am," I fibbed, "but I have so much left to do for the Moon landing."

"Starr, the trip is all planned out. There's nothing else to do but wait for tomorrow." Mom paused and looked at me. "What's really going on?"

I had to tell her the truth.

"The girls are afraid to go on the Moon landing tomorrow," I admitted.

Mom sighed. "I don't understand. They seem so excited. Their parents said they've been having a great time living on the station."

I explained to Mom what they had told me.

"They both think this?" she asked.

I nodded.

"What about the boys?"

"They can't wait," I said.

"Well, I'm not going to force anyone if they're not comfortable. It will be a shame to take the boys but not the girls, though."

At that moment an idea hit me like a meteor. "I think you just gave me an idea," I said.

"What is it?"

"I'm not exactly sure," I continued, "but I think I know a way to help the girls get over their fear. Let's go meet Tia and Mrs. Sosa. We'll need to stop and get Apollo too."

Mom, Apollo, and I met Tia and Mrs. Sosa as they floated into the Zero-G pod. "Welcome back to the station," Mom said to Mrs. Sosa and Tia, giving them both big hugs.

Mrs. Sosa gave Apollo and me hugs too. "I can't even tell you how excited Tia and I are to visit the Moon tomorrow. This is something I've looked forward to my entire life."

"We're excited too," I said. "If it's okay with you, Apollo and I need to steal Tia for a little while."

"By all means," Mrs. Sosa said. "Your mom and I have a lot of planning to go over. Tia has been looking forward to getting back on the station to see you guys."

I smiled and handed Tia a cruiser. The three of us zipped off toward my room.

When we got there, Tia got off and floated over to look through my telescope pointed out at the Moon.

"You remember I told you that the girls are terrified to go to the Moon?" I asked, floating over to her.

Tia looked up, nervously. "Sure," she said.

"Are you positive you don't have any idea why they're suddenly afraid of going to the Moon?"

She peered into the telescope again and shook her head that she didn't know.

"I told you," Apollo said, as if on cue.

"You told me what?" I asked.

"I told you girls aren't tough enough for space." It was perfect.

Tia's head bolted up as if she'd heard a high-pitched noise.

"Excuse me?" she asked.

"I'm not surprised the girls are chickening out. They're not tough enough for the Moon," Apollo said.

Tia looked at me in disbelief. "Starr! Are you going to let him say that?"

"If you had asked me a week ago, I would have told you he was crazy," I said. "But with the girls getting so frightened suddenly, I'm starting to think he might be right."

Tia's jaw just about hit the floor. "You can't be serious?"

"I know, it's crazy," I replied. "But all the boys are ready to go, and the girls don't even want to leave the station. Also, Mom said that if the girls don't go on the Moon walk tomorrow, you and I will have to stay behind with them." I kind of added that last bit to really get her worked up.

"Let me talk with them. They were fine when they were with me in training. I think I can help make them feel safe about it again."

I smiled. "I don't know. They're pretty frightened."

"They're girls," Apollo said. "What do you expect?"

Tia looked like steam might shoot out of her ears. "Let me talk to them."

I smiled. "If you insist."

Chapter 10

THANK APOLLO

The next morning, Tia and I were having breakfast and waiting for the girls to arrive. I hoped my plan had worked.

"I spoke with the girls last night," she said. "They seemed much better. It's a good thing I'm here to calm them down."

I didn't want to get in an argument, so I didn't tell her that I knew she was the reason they were afraid in the first place. "Yeah, it's a really good thing you're here," I replied. I think I rolled my eyes, but I'm not sure.

After breakfast, we all gathered in the tech pod. Professor Will was just about ready for us. It was going to be our biggest mission yet, and I really felt like a part of the crew. Mom pulled me aside and whispered, "I don't know how you did it, but it looks like you saved the mission. I spoke with all the girls' parents this morning, and they're now really excited to go to the Moon."

"Thank Apollo," I said. "He did all the work."

"That's so nice that you two solved the problem together," she said. I tried not to roll my eyes, but I think I probably did. She didn't notice.

Mom addressed the group and explained that we were all going down in three ships. Mom would take the girls, Mrs. Sosa, and Cozzie. Professor Will and Dad would take down the boys, and Kathy would take down the other adults.

All the girls loaded in the ship with Mom and Cozzie. We buckled in, put on our helmets, and Mom fired up the engine.

The huge hatch opened on the side of the station, and then Mom flew the ship out into the black of space. "You are all in for the treat of a lifetime," she said.

She turned the ship toward the Moon. It glowed against the black of space.

"I can't believe how big it is," said Val.

"I can't believe we almost missed this!" Monique declared.

The closer we flew, the more detail I could make out. The craters came into view more clearly, and then we could see large boulders on the surface.

Mom flew along the surface for a while and finally landed the ship softly in the same place we had landed the week before. I could still see the footprints and tire tracks.

Mom shut down the engine, and I said, "Welcome to the Moon, everyone."

Mrs. Sosa looked like she might cry. "Up until last week, no humans had set foot on the Moon since 1972. My dream has come true."

"The best is yet to come," Mom reminded her. She opened the hatch on the back of the ship. We turned and they all looked out in awe at the landscape.

"Unbelievable!" Tia exclaimed.

"Come on," I said. "Follow me."

We lined up at the back of the ship. "Would you like to do the honors?" Mom asked me.

"Sure," I said, turning to look at everyone. "I'm going to count down from three and then we'll all jump off at the same time. Remember that gravity on the Moon is about six times weaker than on Earth. You're going to go much higher when you jump and come down much slower as you fall." Everyone smiled at me — they were ready "Okay, here we go! Three, two, one, JUMP!" We jumped up at the same time and floated in space as if in slow motion. Gently, we returned to the surface, and everyone erupted in shrieks of excitement.

I turned to see the boys and the adults doing the same thing. Mom waved us over toward them. They were all fast learners, and it was fun to see them move around on the Moon's surface. This felt like the start of something. I couldn't help imagining what the Moon would look like in a few years. I could imagine cities on the Moon and people traveling across the surface and flying through the air in Moon planes.

"Congratulations!" Mom said to everyone, after a few more minutes. "You're the first of hopefully many more people to visit the Moon on a vacation. We hope you inspire people to look up at the stars and wonder what it would be like to visit space. Let's be safe today and have fun. We've put together a few activities to help you enjoy your time on the Moon."

"The first activity is the long jump," I said. "As I'm sure you've already realized, you can jump and run much more easily up here than you can on Earth. Everyone will get about twenty minutes to practice and then we'll have a little friendly competition."

We hopped, jumped, and skipped all over the Moon.

It was a complete blast. We took turns trying to jump longer than the person before us. Of course, Apollo and Clark jumped the farthest out of everyone. I didn't mind. I was just happy that the girls came along with the group.

I almost said something to Tia a few times, but she was having such a good time, I decided not to. It was wrong of her to scare the girls and try to make me look bad, but I didn't want to confront her and ruin the day.

A little later, Mom rolled out the rovers. "You can all have some time driving around in the rovers. Have fun, but be safe."

We all split up and piled into different rovers. I ended up with Tia, Cozzie, Monique, and Val. The boys climbed into their own rover and peeled out, sending Moon dust all around.

"It's just like driving a go-kart," I said. "It's a much bumpier ride, though. I try not to get going too fast or the rover becomes hard to control."

We bounced along the surface. After about five

minutes, I let Monique drive. She made a bunch of figure eights on the surface. Then Tia had a turn. She was having the best time. I was happy for her, but I was also a little upset. I wasn't sure how to handle it. She had lied to the girls about me and tried to ruin the mission. We were supposed to be a team.

Chapter 11

THE APOLLO MISSION

After a while, we drove back to the ships.

"Have you seen your brother and the boys?" Mom asked.

"I haven't seen them in a while," I answered.

Mom looked concerned, and so did the other parents. Mom tried calling the boys on the radio, but there wasn't an answer. She called Apollo's phone, but he didn't answer. She texted him, but he didn't respond.

Dad and Professor Will went off in one rover to look for them. Kathy and Mrs. Sosa went off in another. Mom and the other boys' parents were getting more concerned by the minute. Mom took the parents back to one of the ships so they could contact Mrs. Sosa and think of a plan.

Val looked as if she might cry. "I knew this was too dangerous," she said, as her eyes welled with tears.

"I hope they didn't get taken by aliens," Cozzie said.

"Cozzie! That's a terrible thing to say," I said. "There aren't any aliens. It's probably just Apollo trying to be cool and show off again. I bet he will come rolling up the hill any time now."

We waited, but he didn't come rolling up the hill. I was really starting to get worried when Tia pulled me aside and said, "I think I might know where they are."

"How?" I asked.

"Remember when you went on the first Moon mission with your family?"

"Of course," I said.

"I watched the whole video stream from the training center. At one point Apollo asked your mother if he could go down into a crater."

"Yes," I said. "Mom said he couldn't because some of them are really deep and it might be too hard to get out."

"Right," Tia continued. "Later on, Apollo must have forgotten that his helmet camera was on because he was talking to himself. I overheard him saying that he could easily go down into a crater and make it back out."

"Do you think he's in a crater?"

"I think it's worth a look," Tia said, turning on the rover and sliding into the driver's seat. "He's your brother. Which direction do you think he would have gone?"

"My brother would have headed for the deepest crater around," Val said.

"Knowing the two of them, I bet you're right," I said.

I scanned the area to see if we could simply follow their tracks, but there were tracks going every direction by now. It was impossible to tell which ones were theirs.

I texted Mom: *We have a few ideas about where the boys are. Is it okay if we search a bit?*

She texted right back: *Good idea. Make sure to leave*

your phone on. Let me know if you find anything and remember to stay safe.

"Mom said we're good to go."

Tia hit the gas, and I used the GPS on my phone to search for the deepest craters in the area. Tia drove up to the rim of the first crater. It was empty. I felt uneasy. *What if something bad had happened to them?* I wondered.

They weren't in the second crater either. Val was getting more and more upset by the second. I felt the same way, but tried not to show it. It had been at least an hour since anyone had seen them. Their space suits were only designed to support them for about three hours. We had already been on the surface of the Moon for over two. No one said it, but we were all thinking it: we had to find them soon.

We pulled up to the edge of every other large crater in the area and still found nothing. We were just about to turn around and head back to the ships when I caught a glimpse of what looked like their rover way down at the bottom of a massive crater.

"Is that them?" I asked.

"It looks like it!" Val exclaimed, standing on her seat to get a better view. "That's definitely them!" she shouted.

I tried communicating with them on the radio, but there wasn't a signal. Apollo waved his hands, and I could tell he was trying to tell me that he'd killed the battery.

I called Mom. "We've found the boys," I said. "They're way down inside a big crater. I think you'll have to come get them. It looks like their battery is dead."

"Great work, Starr! Stay where you are. I'll be right over. Text me your location."

A few minutes later, Mom arrived in her rover. I pointed toward the boys at the bottom of the crater, and then she took off in that direction.

"I think we saved them," I said.

"That was really scary," Val said. "I was afraid we wouldn't see them again."

"It's lucky that we're such a good team," Tia said.

I tried not to roll my eyes, but it didn't work.

"I owe you an apology," Tia continued. "I told the girls that the Moon wasn't safe."

I didn't say anything.

"I don't know what I was thinking," she said. "I'm supposed to be your partner, and I was working against you. I'm sorry."

"Why did you want to frighten the girls into not going to the Moon?" I asked.

"I was jealous, I guess. You get to be the one up in space doing all the cool stuff, and I'm the one stuck on Earth and training everyone."

"You get to do some pretty cool stuff too," I reminded her. "You're in the middle of a rescue mission on the Moon."

"I'll try not to get jealous," she said. "Do you forgive me?"

"Of course," I said. I was glad she apologized, and I wanted to believe her.

Just then, Mom's rover reappeared towing Apollo's. She gave us a thumbs-up and pointed back toward the direction of the ships.

Later on, when we were back in the station, Apollo asked me how we found him. "Tia remembered that you had wanted to go in a crater on our first Moon walk, but Mom wouldn't let you," I said. "We figured you just had to try it. Am I right?"

"I don't know what I was thinking. We were really lucky that you guys found us. I wasn't paying attention to the rover's power supply. The battery completely died on us."

"Why didn't you answer your phone? Mom tried to call and text you."

"I forgot it on the station," he said.

Of course you did, I thought. "We were super-excited when we found you. I was really afraid, Apollo."

"It was really scary," he said. "And I was wrong."

"About what?" I asked.

"The Moon is clearly not too dangerous for girls. It turns out it's too dangerous for me, though."

I smiled. "Yeah, I guess you're right. Next time just stay by me, and I'll keep you safe."

"Very funny," he said, smiling.

"Also, very true," I said.

ABOUT THE AUTHOR

Raymond Bean is the best-selling author of the *Benji Franklin*, *Sweet Farts*, and *School Is a Nightmare* books. He teaches by day and writes by night. He lives in New York with his wife, two children, and a Cockapoo named Lily. His bags are packed for the day when space-cations become a reality.

ABOUT THE ILLUSTRATOR

Matthew Vimislik is an illustrator and game designer working in Rochester, NY. He lives with his wife, two cats, and possibly a family of Black-billed Cuckoo birds that has made a nest in his meticulously preened hair.

STARR'S GUIDE
TO SPACE TRAVEL

APOLLO — My mom and dad named my older brother Apollo after the Apollo space missions that landed the first humans on the Moon.

AQUAPONICS — Fish and plants live together in an aquaponic system. That means a place where fish and plants are grown together. The fish waste provides nutrients to the plants, and the plants help purify the water. It's how we grow food and raise fish on our space station.

ASTEROID — Asteroids are rocks floating in space. They can be hundreds of miles across or as small as a few feet long.

COMET — Comets are like dirty snowballs in space. They're made of ice and dust.

COSMO — My little brother's name is Cosmo. Mom and Dad got his name from the word "cosmos," which means "the universe." It's a good name because sometimes my brother thinks the universe revolves around him.

CRATER — A bowl-shaped area on the Moon. Asteroids and meteors crash into the Moon, causing craters.

MICROGRAVITY — The word "micro" means "very small." Gravity is the force that holds us to the ground. In space, gravity is not as strong, so "microgravity" basically means "small gravity." When you see astronauts floating around in space, it's because of microgravity. Microgravity is so much fun! You have to experience it one day!

ORBIT — The way something goes around an object in space is called its orbit. The Moon is in orbit around Earth.

SPACE-CATION — Tia and I pretty much made the word up. It's basically the words "space" and "vacation" put together.

STABILIZER — A stabilizer is used to keep something steady or stable. In space we use them to hold us in place. If we didn't have them, we'd float all over the place!

VELCRO — Velcro is two strips covered in tiny loops or hooks. We use tons of Velcro to hold things in place in space. Without Velcro, our stuff would float all over the station.

ZERO-G — This is basically the same thing as microgravity, when you don't feel gravity and you float. Sometimes people call this weightlessness. Most people think of it as floating, but it feels more like you are falling.

FAR-OUT QUESTIONS

1. Starr and her family travel to the Moon. On the Moon, gravity is not as strong as it is on Earth. Imagine you had the opportunity to travel across the surface of the Moon. How would it be different than traveling on Earth? Do you think you would enjoy traveling on the Moon?

2. In chapter nine, Starr says, "I think I know a way to help the girls get over their fear." What fear is Starr talking about? How does she help them get over their fear?

3. In the book, Starr and the crew visit the Moon! Humans have not set foot on the Moon since 1972. Why do you think it's taken so long to return to the Moon? Do you think people will land on the Moon again? If so, when? If not, why?

INTERGALACTIC IDEAS

1   The author chose to write *Journey to the Moon* as a chapter book. Do you think the story could be told as a picture book? If so, how would it be different? How would it be the same? Try writing a scene from the book as a picture book. Include an illustration.

2   Starr's older brother, Apollo, thinks girls aren't tough enough for space. How does Starr prove him wrong? Use examples from the book in your answer.

3   Starr and the crew use cruisers to move around the station. Imagine you were asked to invent a new form of transportation to be used in microgravity. Describe your invention and how it would make life in space easier.

Check out
some *space-tastic*
websites at
www.FactHound.com

Just type in the book ID: 9781496536167
and prepare to blast off!